The Sunflower That Went FLOP

by Joy Cowley

Mrs. Brown
had a sunflower
growing by the wall.

It was straight and tall,
and yellow as the sun.

The people passing by
looked at it and said,
"What a beauty!"

2

Day after day,
the sunflower stood tall
by the wall,
under the hot sun.

Then, one afternoon,
suddenly,
the sunflower
went
FLOP.

3

"What a shame!"
said the people passing by.

"Oh, my poor flower,"
cried Mrs. Brown.
And she ran to Mr. Brown.

4

"What is it, my love?" he asked.

"Our big yellow sunflower went FLOP," she said.

Mr. Brown only laughed.
"Don't get in a tizz," he said.
"I'll fix it.
I can fix anything."

5

Mr. Brown opened up his fix-it bag
and got out some sticky tape.
"This should do it," he said.

He went stick, stick, stick,
and stood the sunflower up
by the wall again.

"What a clever man
you are," said Mrs. Brown.

Mr. Brown put away
his fix-it bag.
"Think nothing of it,
my love," he said.
"It was easy."

That should
do it!

6

The sun was hot all day,
and the next afternoon,
suddenly,
the sunflower
went
FLOP.

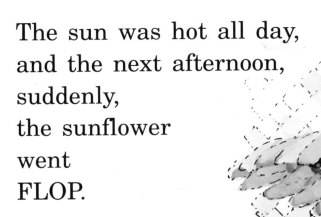

"What a shame!"
said the people passing by.

Mrs. Brown saw it and cried,
"My poor sunflower!"
And she called Mr. Brown.

"What is it, my love?" he asked.

"Our sunflower went FLOP again,"
she said.

Mr. Brown only laughed.
"Don't get in a tizz," he said.
"I'll fix it.
I can fix anything."

He opened his fix-it bag
and got out
a needle and string.

"This should do it,"
he said. He went
stitch, stitch, stitch,
and stitched
the sunflower
up by the wall.

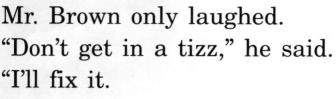

"What a clever man you are," said Mrs. Brown.

Mr. Brown put away his fix-it bag.

"Think nothing of it, my love," he said. "It was easy."

That's better.

The sun was hot
all day, and the
next afternoon,
suddenly,
the sunflower
went
FLOP.

"What a shame!"
said the people passing by.

"Oh dear, oh dear,"
cried Mrs. Brown.

"What is it, my love?"
said Mr. Brown.

"Our sunflower has gone FLOP
again," said Mrs. Brown.

Mr. Brown only laughed.
"Don't get in a tizz," he said.
"I'll fix it. I can fix anything."

He opened up his fix-it bag
and got out a hammer and nails.
"This should do it," he said.

He went hammer, hammer, hammer,
and stood the sunflower
up by the wall again.

"What a clever man you are,"
said Mrs. Brown.

Mr. Brown put away his fix-it bag.
"Think nothing of it, my love,"
he said. "It was easy."

The sun was hot all day,
and the next afternoon,
suddenly,
the sunflower
went
FLOP.

"What a shame!"
said the people passing by.

Mrs. Brown looked at it
and shook her head.
Then she went to tell Mr. Brown.
"It's done it again," she said.

"Oh," said Mr. Brown.
"Blow!" said Mr. Brown.

"Can you fix it?"
asked Mrs. Brown.

"Of course," said Mr. Brown.
"I can fix anything.
But let's do it in the morning.
I'm always best at fixing things
in the morning."

13

That night,
it rained
and rained
and rained.

The sunflower
drank and drank
and drank.

It grew straight
and tall again.

14

The next morning,
the people passing by
stopped to look.
"What a beauty!" they said.

Mrs. Brown went
to the window.
"My sunflower!" she cried.

15

She ran to Mr. Brown and hugged him.
"I don't know how you did it," she said.
"You fixed it. You really fixed it.
What a *clever* man you are."

But Mr. Brown only laughed.
"Think nothing of it, my love," he said.
"It was easy."

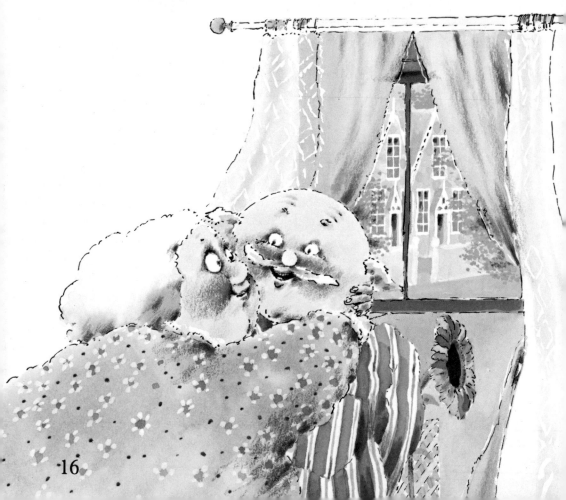